Pete the Cat

I Love My White Shoes

Art by James Dean
(creator of Pete the Cat)

Story by Eric Litwin

HARPER

An Imprint of HarperCollinsPublishers

Pete the Cat was walking down the
street in his brand-new white shoes.
Pete loved his white shoes so much,
he sang this song:

Oh no!

Pete stepped in a large pile of ......

strawberries!

What color did it turn his shoes?

Did Pete cry?
Goodness, no!

He kept walking along and singing his song.

"I love my
red shoes,
I love my
red shoes,
I love my
red shoes."

Oh no!
Pete stepped in a
large pile of ......

blueberries!

What color did it turn his shoes?

Did Pete cry?
Goodness, no!

He kept walking along and singing his song.

"I love my
blue shoes,
I love my
blue shoes,
I love my
blue shoes."

Oh no!

Pete stepped in a
large puddle of......

mud!

What color did it turn his shoes?

Did Pete cry?
Goodness, no!

He kept walking along and singing his song.

"I love my
    brown shoes,
I love my
    brown shoes,
I love my
    brown shoes."

and all the brown,
and all the blue,
and all the red
were washed away.

What color were
his shoes again?

WHITE

But now they were WET.

Did Pete cry?
Goodness, no!

He kept walking along and singing his song.

The moral of Pete's story is:
No matter what you step in,
keep walking along and
singing your song ......

because it's all good.

This book began as a simple dream of Eric and James's.
Then the dream began to grow with help from some very
exceptional people. We are grateful to: Elizabeth Dulemba for
artist direction; Michael Levine for music production;
Marla Zafft for book design; Bobby Slotkin for legal counsel;
Karin Wilson from Page and Palette Bookstore
for sharing our book with HarperCollins.

Pete the Cat: I Love My White Shoes
Copyright © 1999 by James Dean (for the character of Pete the Cat)
Copyright © 2008 by James Dean and Eric Litwin.
All rights reserved. Printed in the United States of America.
No part of this book may be used or reproduced in any manner whatsoever
without written permission except in the case of brief quotation embodied
in critical articles and reviews. For information address HarperCollins Children's Books,
a division of HarperCollins Publishers, 195 Broadway, New York, NY 10007.
www.harpercollinschildrens.com

Library of Congress catalog card number: 2009928950
ISBN 978-0-06-190622-0 (trade bdg.) — ISBN 978-0-06-190623-7 (lib. bdg.)

14 15 16 17 18 SCP 30 29 28 27 26 25 24 23 22 21

❖

First HarperCollins edition, 2010
Originally published in 2008 by Blue Whisker Press, LLC, Atlanta, GA